A NOTE ABOUT THE STORY

Not long ago, Marti Stone spent a year in Switzerland with her family. Outside their chalet grew a large, elegant fir tree, which they soon gave a name and a personality all its own. If it didn't actually sing to Marti, it certainly did speak to her. And it spoke of the profound love and respect that the Swiss have for the natural beauty of their country— a country in which a centuries-old tradition of wood-carving can exist comfortably with an equally venerable tradition of care for the environment.

Even after Marti returned to her home in Vermont, that tree still called to her. So when she came upon this Swiss folktale about a man and the magical wood he carves, she knew she must follow her instinct to its end: the text for her first picture book.

That left Barry Root's breathtaking alpine illustrations to complete the magic of the story. Sharp with the rarefied light of the mountain air, these paintings make you feel as if at any moment you will hear a faraway tree breaking into song.

Tomie dePaola, Creative Director
WHITEBIRD BOOKS

THE SINGING FIR TREE

A Swiss folktale retold by **Marti Stone**

illustrated by **Barry Root**

A WHITEBIRD BOOK
G. P. Putnam's Sons
New York

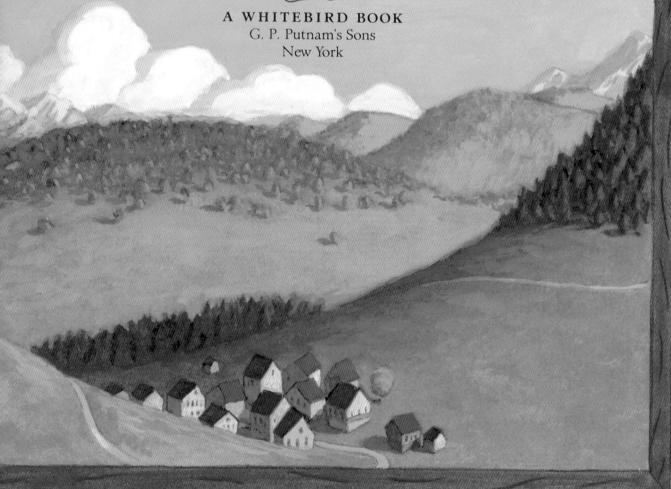

Text copyright © 1992 by Marti Stone
Illustrations copyright © 1992 by Barry Root
All rights reserved. This book, or parts thereof, may not be reproduced
in any form without permission in writing from the publisher.
G. P. Putnam's Sons, a division of The Putnam & Grosset Group,
200 Madison Avenue, New York, NY 10016. Published simultaneously in Canada.
Printed in Hong Kong by South China Printing Co. (1988) Ltd.
Book design by Gunta Alexander.   The text is set in Administer.
Library of Congress Cataloging-in-Publication Data
Stone, Marti. The singing fir tree : a Swiss folktale /
retold by Marti Stone : illustrated by Barry Root.   p.   cm.   "A Whitebird book."
Summary: In his quest to find the perfect wood for his masterpiece,
a woodcarver tries to cut down the town's beloved singing fir tree.
[1. Folklore—Switzerland.] I. Root, Barry, ill. II. Title.
PZ8.1.S8596 Si 1992 398.24'2'09494—dc20 [e] 89-33400 CIP AC
ISBN 0-399-22207-3
1. 3   5   7   9   10   8   6   4   2
First Impression

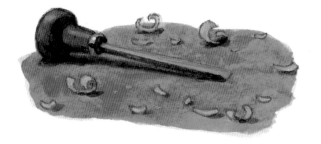

Pierre the woodcarver was restless. The toys and boxes and candlesticks he made were always in demand by the townspeople, but he wanted to carve one special work that would make him famous all over Switzerland.

Pierre didn't know what he would carve, but he knew that if he were to create a masterpiece, he needed to live in a quiet village high in the mountains where the finest trees grew.

So one day he filled his backpack with his tools and belongings and headed up the twisted mountain trails on his horse until he found a village that had work for a woodcarver.

"You can put your workshop upstairs," said the baker, "and you may have all the bread you want, if you will make new shelves and flower boxes for my bakery."

Pierre finished the work quickly and the baker was so happy with what he had done that he sent his friends to Pierre. Pierre had lots of work, but he did not forget why he had come.

Each afternoon he walked through the forest, searching for the tree with the right wood. Cedric, the baker's son, began to go with Pierre on his afternoon walks.

"What will you make?" Cedric asked.

"That I cannot tell you because I do not know myself, but it will be something big and grand."

Just then the village clock rang and Pierre stopped short.

"I will make a beautiful carved tower to cover the clock. People will come from all over the mountains and the valleys to see my fine work."

Cedric went to the shop every day to watch Pierre carving his model for the clock tower. Sometimes he brought hot buns with him and Pierre made them tea. On other days Pierre did not even look up when Cedric came in. Then Cedric watched from the corner of the room and hummed quietly to keep himself from asking questions.

One night when Pierre was working late, he heard the song that Cedric hummed, coming from the forest.

Cedric? he thought. But no, it couldn't be. He went out onto the balcony to listen more clearly.

"I must be imagining things," Pierre murmured. And he went back to his bench.

The next morning, Pierre heard the song from the forest again. I must find out who is making such a beautiful sound, he thought. So he climbed up the steep mountain trail higher and higher, following the song. But the wind confused him and he could not find anyone singing.

After that, Pierre heard the music often. Finally he talked to Cedric.

"This is foolish, but is there someone singing in the forest?"

Cedric smiled. "Come with me," he said, and he led Pierre along the brook and up to a field half hidden by the forest. In the corner was an old fir tree, bent crooked by the wind. It was singing as if all the birds of the mountain were in its branches.

"When the wind is right, it carries the song down to the village," he told Pierre.

Pierre listened and then went over to the thick trunk and touched it. In all his years as a woodcarver, he had never felt wood so soft.

"At last I have found what I have been looking for. The wood for my masterpiece."

Cedric looked horrified.

"No," he said. "You cannot cut this tree down. It is part of our village. It has been here forever. It sang to my grandfather when he was a boy."

"No, of course, I won't cut it down," Pierre said quickly. But he was already thinking about holding the wood in his hands.

After that Pierre could not work for thinking about the tree. His tools lay on the bench while his hands tapped the rhythm of the song. What a tower he could make. He did not want to take the tree from the forest, but no other tree would do. He decided to approach the villagers.

"No! Never!" they said. "We would love to have a beautiful clock tower, but you must find another tree."

But Pierre had made up his mind, and he thought of a way to get the tree and keep the villagers from knowing. He went to market and bought a herd of the best Brown Swiss cows. He hung a bell from each cow's neck and listened as the bells clanged whenever the cows moved. He led the herd up to the field in the forest. No one will hear the music of one fir tree above the sound of so many bells, Pierre thought, and no one will miss the tree before I make my masterpiece. When they see my tower, they will forget all about the tree.

But whenever the wind was right and the tree sang, the cows stopped grazing to listen, and their bells were silent.

Pierre was disappointed. He tried to forget about the tree and work on other things. But the more he tried to forget, the more he dreamed of working with its magic wood. Then he had a new idea.

He waited for a windy, stormy night. Then he picked up his ax with one hand and a lantern with the other and climbed up to the field. He would cut down the tree and let the villagers think that it had fallen in the storm. But with the first cut, the tree oozed a thick, sticky pitch which covered the ax and Pierre's hands. It was impossible to continue or even carry the lantern, so Pierre stumbled home in the dark, his hands so sticky he couldn't carve for a week.

Pierre was angry. "This must stop! I must have my special tree," he said to himself as he looked out toward the forest. His horse was grazing below. Pierre went to the back of his shop and got a thick piece of rope. While the villagers were at their noon meal, he led his horse up to the field.

"Now, friend, the two of us should be able to take down one old tree." And he tied one end of the rope to the saddle and one to the tree. "Let's pull!"

The horse turned to obey, but then he stopped and lifted his head. The tree was singing in the wind. Pierre tugged again, but the horse was listening to the music and would not move. Then Pierre heard voices rising up from the village. The children were singing the tree's song while they played. Pierre heard Cedric's voice clearly.

"What am I doing?" he said. "This song is more beautiful than any clock tower I could carve." When the music stopped, he untied the rope and led his horse out of the field. But he found his path blocked by some branches which had dropped from the tree. He picked them up and carried them back to his shop.

The next morning Pierre took the branches to his bench. Just as he began working, Cedric came in bringing him some freshly baked bread.

"You are working again! What are you going to make?" Cedric asked.

"That I cannot tell you because I do not know myself," Pierre told him. "We must see what my hands will carve."

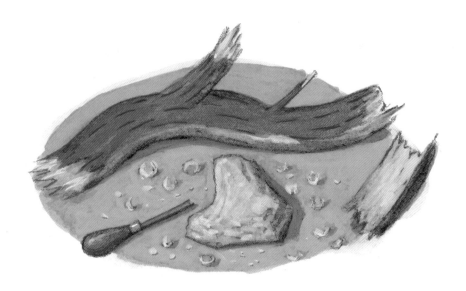

In only a few hours he had a pile of wooden birds in front of him. "Gifts from the tree," he said. "Choose one for yourself and take one to each of the children."

That evening the wind carried the familiar melody to Pierre's room. But the voices sounded different. He went out onto the balcony to listen. The children were gathered around their wooden birds and the birds were singing the fir tree's sweet song. And from the field up in the forest, a crooked fir tree sang back.